Little Bear's
Numbers

For Bryan and Margaret

Old Bear and Friends by Jane Hissey in Red Fox

Old Bear Little Bear's Trousers Little Bear Lost
Jolly Tall Jolly Snow Ruff Hoot
Old Bear and His Friends Old Bear Tales Little Bear's Dragon
Little Bear's Alphabet Old Bear's All-Together Painting

LITTLE BEAR'S NUMBERS
A RED FOX BOOK 0 09 943337 0

First published in Great Britain by Hutchinson,
an imprint of Random House Children's Books

Hutchinson edition published 2001
Red Fox edition published 2002

1 3 5 7 9 10 8 6 4 2

© Jane Hissey 2001

Red Fox Books are published by Random House Children's Books,
61–63 Uxbridge Road, London W5 5SA,
a division of The Random House Group Ltd,
in Australia by Random House Australia (Pty) Ltd,
20 Alfred Street, Milsons Point, Sydney, NSW 2061, Australia,
in New Zealand by Random House New Zealand Ltd,
18 Poland Road, Glenfield, Auckland 10, New Zealand,
and in South Africa by Random House (Pty) Ltd,
Endulini, 5A Jubilee Road, Parktown 2193, South Africa

THE RANDOM HOUSE GROUP Limited Reg. No. 954009
www.randomhouse.co.uk

A CIP catalogue record for this book is available from the British Library.

Printed in Singapore by Tien Wah Press PTE Ltd

Little Bear's Numbers

JANE HISSEY

RED FOX

1 2 3 4 5 6 7 8 9 10

1
one

1 sock

1 2 3 4 5 6 7 8 9 10

There is one candle on Ruff's birthday cake.

1 **2** 3 4 5 6 7 8 9 10

2
two

2 buckets

There are two shadows dancing on the wall.

1 2 **3** 4 5 6 7 8 9 10

3
three

3 bears

1 2 **3** 4 5 6 7 8 9 10

Here are three naughty toys jumping on the bed.

1 2 3 4 5 6 7 8 9 10

four

4 boots

1 2 3 4 5 6 7 8 9 10

Where is Dog hiding his four rubber bones?

1 2 3 4 **5** 6 7 8 9 10

5
five

5 biscuits

Here are five bears in a basket.

1 2 3 4 5 6 7 8 9 10

6
six

6 candles

1 2 3 4 5 6 7 8 9 10

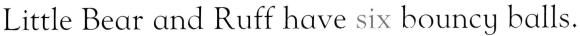

Little Bear and Ruff have six bouncy balls.

1 2 3 4 5 6 7 8 9 10

7
seven

7 books

1 2 3 4 5 6 **7** 8 9 10

Can you see seven hats?

1 2 3 4 5 6 7 8 9 10

8
eight

8 paintbrushes

1 2 3 4 5 6 7 8 9 10

Old Bear is catching eight pieces of pink paper.

1 2 3 4 5 6 7 8 9 10

9
nine

9 puzzle pieces

1 2 3 4 5 6 7 8 **9** 10

There are nine blue bubbles floating in the air.

1 2 3 4 5 6 7 8 9 10

10
ten

10 sticks

Ruff is driving his train over ten coloured pencils.

The toys are playing hide-and-seek. Let's help
Old Bear count to ten.

Can you guess how many friends he will find?

How many different things can you count?

Toys, hats, flags, bricks, bears, noses and ears!

More Red Fox picture books
for you to enjoy

ELMER
by David McKee 0099697203

MUMMY LAID AN EGG!
by Babette Cole 0099299119

THE RUNAWAY TRAIN
by Benedict Blathwayt 0099385716

DOGGER
by Shirley Hughes 009992790X

WHERE THE WILD THINGS ARE
by Maurice Sendak 0099408392

OLD BEAR
by Jane Hissey 0099265761

MISTER MAGNOLIA
by Quentin Blake 0099400421

ALFIE GETS IN FIRST
by Shirley Hughes 0099855607

OI! GET OFF OUR TRAIN
by John Burningham 009985340X

GORGEOUS!
by Caroline Castle and Sam Childs 0099400766